Order this book online at www.trafford.com
or email orders@trafford.com

Most Trafford titles are also available at major online book retailers.

www.trafford.com

North America & international
toll-free: 844 688 6899 (USA & Canada)
fax: 812 355 4082

Our mission is to efficiently provide the world's finest, most comprehensive book publishing service, enabling every author to experience success. To find out how to publish your book, your way, and have it available worldwide, visit us online at www.trafford.com

Because of the dynamic nature of the Internet, any web addresses or links contained in this book may have changed since publication and may no longer be valid. The views expressed in this work are solely those of the author and do not necessarily reflect the views of the publisher, and the publisher hereby disclaims any responsibility for them.

Any people depicted in stock imagery provided by Getty Images are models, and such images are being used for illustrative purposes only.
Certain stock imagery © Getty Images.

ISBN: 978-1-6987-1118-8(sc)
ISBN: 978-1-6987-1119-5(sc)

Print information available on the last page.

Trafford rev. 02/24/2022

The Adventures of

Spotty
and
Sunny

Book 7: A Fun Learning Series for Kids

COVID-19 Virus. Char Man.
At home and bored. No school.

Author/ Pharmacist
Saisnath Baijoo.

Mom and dad are in a hurry. "Good morning my loves. Your father and I are late again for work at our pharmacy. Grandpa is spending the day with you. Come quickly for a group hug. Remember, your classes are online because of this Covid virus. Bye, love you all. Be safe."

Jordi replies to mom, but she does not hear.

Jas is sad. "We are all bored at home. Why can't we go to school? I miss my friends. School is fun. Learning is fun in school."

Davin jumps up and down on the couch near
sleeping Grandpa causing him to fall on the floor.
Everyone laughs except sleepy Grandpa.

Dominic hugs Grandpa. "Grandpa, I am super bored
at home. Can we go to see Spotty and Sunny?"

Sleepy Grandpa scratches his hands for a moment. He yawns. "No
son. It is not a good idea. Your teachers and parents spoke to you all
about the Covid 19 virus. We can zoom online with Spotty today."

Dominic shows a sad face. "Now, I really understand how a caged bird feels."

Grandpa hugs Dominic. "Kids, remember our visit to McDonald's farm with your mom, dad and many friends?"

Everyone is excited. "Yes Grandpa. It was fun."

Everyone moves closer to him. They enjoy his exciting and funny stories.

Sleepy Grandpa continues. "Wasn't visiting the farm fun? Outdoors is fun. You saw so many different animals like pigs, cows, and sheep. You liked the colorful fishes. You ate bananas, and fruits from the trees. You all got excited when you saw 20 baby chicks pecking at their food. You all sneaked up quietly near them. You were singing and playing the counting game. You sang together. Now, there are 1,2,3,4,5,6,7,8,9,10,11,12,13,14,15,16,17,18,19,20."

Mom joined in the fun. "What about even number from 1 to 20?"

Davin quietly says. "Yes. I can. They are 2, 4,6,8,10,12,14,16,18 and 20."

Dominic boasts. "I know the odd numbers. They are 1,3,5,7,9,11,13,15,17and 19.

Jordi knocks his chest. "Mine, mine. All these chicks are mine. I have fourteen are black or white but six have many colors." Everyone laughs.

Sleepy Grandpa laughs. "All of a sudden, Jordi ran to hold them. Mother hen was afraid for her babies. She ran quickly towards her baby chicks to protect them. She pecked him. He started to cry."

Jas was sad. "Oh. Yes, I remember. Some were yellow. Some were white. Some were brown. Some were black. Some were spotted colors with red, black, yellow, and white. We wanted to play with the babies. Mother hen was angry. Aww, their mom pecked me."

Dominic and Davin were laughing at Jas. They rushed to play with the baby chicks. They got pecked.

Grandpa is amused. "Their mom was afraid. She was only protecting her babies. She covered them with her huge wings. All twenty babies were under her colorful wings. Their father stood near them. He tried to peck everyone. My Grandkids were afraid. Jordi ran East. Jas ran West. Dominic ran North. Davin ran South."

Jordi is sad." Grandpa, it was not funny. We were afraid."

Grandpa laughs. "Mom were protecting her baby chicks. They are safe under her wings.

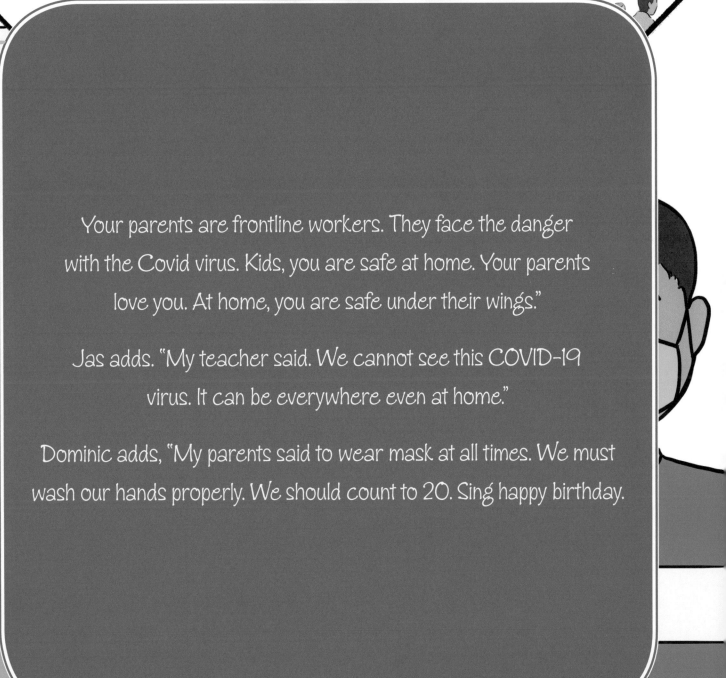

Your parents are frontline workers. They face the danger with the Covid virus. Kids, you are safe at home. Your parents love you. At home, you are safe under their wings."

Jas adds. "My teacher said. We cannot see this COVID-19 virus. It can be everywhere even at home."

Dominic adds, "My parents said to wear mask at all times. We must wash our hands properly. We should count to 20. Sing happy birthday.

6 feet

Grandpa adds, "For now, we must at least six feet away from our friends. No hugs, kisses or rub your eyes."

Grandpa smiles. "Come kids. We have a few minutes before your classes. We can zoom with Spotty, Sunny, and family."

Grandpa speaks to Spotty. Everyone waves at Spotty, Sunny, Miss Snapper and Mr. Tam.

Davin shouts. "Hello. Are you in school? Are you bored at home?"

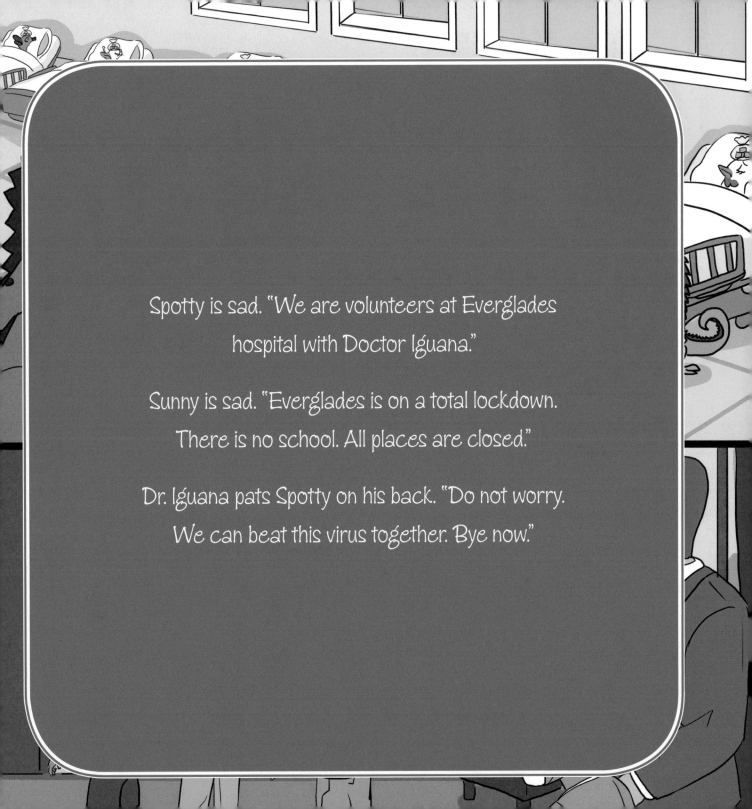

Spotty is sad. "We are volunteers at Everglades hospital with Doctor Iguana."

Sunny is sad. "Everglades is on a total lockdown. There is no school. All places are closed."

Dr. Iguana pats Spotty on his back. "Do not worry. We can beat this virus together. Bye now."

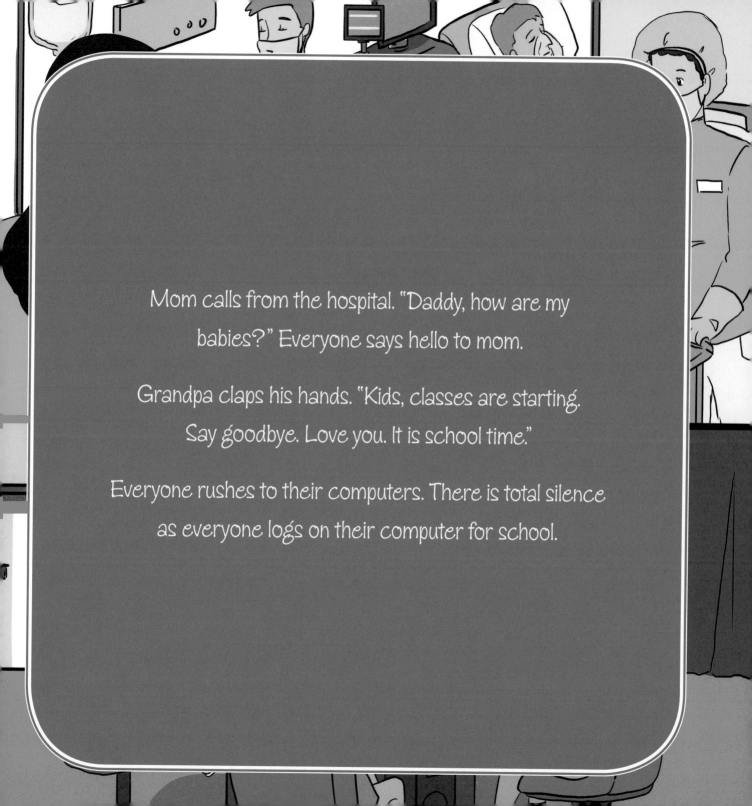

Mom calls from the hospital. "Daddy, how are my babies?" Everyone says hello to mom.

Grandpa claps his hands. "Kids, classes are starting. Say goodbye. Love you. It is school time."

Everyone rushes to their computers. There is total silence as everyone logs on their computer for school.

Grandpa covers his face with his big hat and goes to sleep.
After classes sleeping Grandpa awakes. He plays music and
dances with his grandchildren. They are happy and safe.

Thank you for your order on sbaijao.com

Text me at (786) 223-2563

Follow me on Facebook, Instagram, and Twitter

Printed in the United States
by Baker & Taylor Publisher Services